K. M. Peyton

Froggett's Revenge

Illustrated by Maureen Bradley

OCE96

PUFFIN BOOKS
in association with
Oxford University Press

To Christopher

PUFFIN BOOKS

Published by the Penguin Group
27 Wrights Lane, London W8 5TZ, England
Viking Penguin Inc., 40 West 23rd Street, New York, New York 10010, USA
Penguin Books Australia Ltd, Ringwood, Victoria, Australia
Penguin Books Canada Ltd, 2801 John Street, Markham, Ontario, Canada L3R 1B4
Penguin Books (NZ) Ltd, 182–190 Wairau Road, Auckland 10, New Zealand

Penguin Books Ltd, Registered Offices: Harmondsworth, Middlesex, England

First published by Oxford University Press 1985
Published in Puffin Books 1987
3 5 7 9 10 8 6 4 2

Made and printed in Great Britain by
Richard Clay Ltd, Bungay, Suffolk
Typeset in 11/13 Photina

Denny crouched low behind the stone wall, his heart thumping with sheer terror, loud – it seemed to him – as his dad's diesel. He could not see Wayne coming, only hear Wayne's mother saying all the usual things at the front door of his house, like 'Don't you dare call in the sweet-shop before you get to school – that money is for swimming remember,' and 'Don't forget to tell Miss Randall that you can't stay for team practice on Friday. You've got to catch the bus to go down to your gran's.'

Wayne was shortly going to pass along the road in front of Denny and if he happened to look sideways into the footpath that ran off it up to Moorcroft's farm he was going to see Denny. Denny's cover was sparse, not to mention uncomfortable: a patch of high thistles and a few clumps of long grass smelling of dogs.

If Wayne walked past without seeing him, Denny knew that he would almost die of relief. It would be as gorgeous as Christmas stockings and ginger fudge cake and looking at Mr Parker's traction engine collection all rolled into one. It would be like waking up and remembering it was your birthday. I hate Wayne, Denny was thinking – hating so hard that the long grass seemed to quiver with his hate. If Wayne could catch some spotty disease and die, or if his father's job was moved to Timbuctoo, Denny thought it would be like a great black cloud rolling away from his horizon.

He crouched lower into the grass as Wayne approached. He could hear Wayne's expensive trainers padding on the tarmac. He held his breath. He did not dare look up. You always had the feeling, if you shut your eyes, that somehow the other person would not see you. The padding came and went. He could not believe his luck. His body had the shakes, doubled up for so long – but more with fright than cramp. He was frightened to death of Wayne. Wayne made his whole life a misery.

Cautiously he limped out of his hiding place and peered over the wall. Wayne was walking away from him, quite a long way down the road. Once Wayne was round the bend, it would be safe to start walking. Denny felt the cramps getting better, and an uncommon optimism took over from his usual fears. Perhaps his new idea for avoiding Wayne, having worked today, could prove a winner. It was simple enough. Instead of walking straight to school, passing Wayne's house on the way, (when Wayne always came out to get him,) he had left home at the usual time, as his mother insisted, and, instead of going straight he had taken a footpath up to the farm, round the top of the hill past the Moorcroft's wood and down again to the road in a big loop. Doing this, he had timed it so that he could come back to the road just as Wayne was leaving his house. Hiding behind the wall, waiting until he had gone, had worked.

Denny slung his school-bag over his shoulder and set off down the road feeling pleased with himself.

He was cheerful by nature, considering what he had to bear with, like being called Dennis, and only being half the size of nearly everyone else in his class. His parents called him Denny, and he was always wishing it had been Danny, which was a pretty smart name, to his mind. He pretended to himself that he was Danny, and tall and tough to match, but pretending didn't really work. His surname was Froggett, and a lot of people – even some of the teachers – called him Tadpole. Wayne's surname was

MacFarlane. Denny thought that was a good name. No one called Wayne anything funny.

The road to school was grass fields and woods on one side, and houses on the other. The school was on the houses' side, where the road met a busier road which ran down to the river and the main part of the town. Most of the kids lived in the town and walked up from the other way. There was nobody but Wayne who lived down Denny's road, so Denny was on his own.

But today, thrilled by his clever trick, Denny skipped past the last house in the road and came to the school wall.

'Frogslegs! Got you!'

Wayne, twice Denny's size, vaulted over the wall and landed on Denny's back like a cowboy rider dropping on to his horse from the corral rails. Denny went down with a scrunch and Wayne got hold of his arms and twisted them up behind his back so that he could not even wriggle and knelt on his bottom with his beefy knees squashing Denny flat.

'Come on, Dennis Frogslegs, say what a slimy toad I am, what a sloppy, gloopy mess of frogspawn, what a wally, what a . . .' All the usual stuff – Denny had suffered it for what he considered far too long. The only way out was to repeat all Wayne's accusations, agreeing to them, admitting how utterly lowly and hopeless he was, then Wayne would smirk and let him up by degrees, giving him a few pinches and Chinese burns on the way, his great hams circling Denny's skinny wrists without difficulty. When he was up, the top of Denny's head was on a level with Wayne's armpits. Once, in a rash moment he had pointed out the misfortune of having his nose at this level because of the smell, but he had learnt quite soon that it did not pay to be witty with a larger man. These days, the quicker he agreed to all the insults the quicker the whole miserable business was over with.

'See you after school,' Wayne said cheerfully, when he finally let him go.

No one had seen the incident in the backyard. Everyone was trooping in the front way.

Denny, after his cheerfulness at the clever plan he

had used earlier, now felt as squashed in spirit as he did in body. He could not see any way out of getting bullied. Once, after he had complained of feeling sick for several days and not wanting to go to school, his mother had suspected the truth and gone to Wayne's parents and complained. That had been worse than any of Wayne's thumps, Wayne and his family denying that any such thing could possibly happen and his mother coming back confused and upset. Denny's father had got cross too, saying even if Denny was a little 'un, it was something he had to learn to live with and he must stand on his own feet.

'But he gets knocked off his own feet,' his mother pointed out. She wanted to come to school with him but this was a worse idea still. Denny, in horror, had stopped complaining about feeling sick. In their school, hardly any mothers came, certainly not in the ten-year-old classes. The town was very small, bypassed by busy traffic, with lollipop ladies anyway where it mattered. Imagine his mother coming to the gates! Since she had got so upset, Denny had learned to hide his fears from her. Besides, other kids got done over by Wayne and they didn't complain. Wayne was very good at soccer, being so large and aggressive, and most of them wanted to be good friends with him, to be part of his group. Denny never ever wanted to be friends with Wayne, although he often dreamed of how lovely it would be to be bigger than everyone else, and smart and clever so that everyone picked him first in teams. No, he would be the captain, doing the picking. The only prize he had ever won was the charity Knobbly Knees competition at the school fete. He wasn't good at anything much, although he tried. He had quite a few friends but no one special at school. There was a girl along the road who went to another school, and she knew about Wayne, and had given Denny a huge hat-pin out of her great-grandmother's button box, and told him to jab it in. But it was difficult to carry it about without jabbing it in himself, and he hadn't tried it yet. He kept it in a milk-bottle behind the spare tractor tyre in his dad's barn.

All the same, the idea – of leaving home and taking the path round by the woods and getting back to the road after Wayne had left and gone – seemed better than most. If he took longer, he thought Wayne would get tired of waiting for him. It would make him late. Even if it made him late, Denny thought it would be better to be late than mashed again.

So next day he set off at the right time and nipped up the footpath as before. From the top of the hill he could see the row of houses below him, his own at the end of the row, farthest from the school. He could see Wayne's front door, painted red. The footpath ran the same way as the road for a bit, but higher up the hill, with fields between. On the other side of it there was a rambly wood which covered the top of the hill.

Denny walked slowly. The slower the better. The footpath was overgrown and the grass wet, soaking the legs of his jeans. The big wood was silent, but Denny was startled suddenly by the urgent fluttering

of pigeons flying up in alarm out of the trees, and the sound of cracking branches. He stopped and peered into the dark shade and undergrowth, but could see nothing. The wood went silent again, yet he had a sense of something watching him. He stood waiting. He knew the wood quite well and played in it often and was not afraid of it. But as he stood there he felt strongly that something was different today. Something had frightened the birds. Nothing stirred now,

yet he imagined he could hear heavy, animal breathing. Or was it the wind playing tricks? No, there was no wind. The feeling was so strong that he forgot the red front door. He stared into the wood.

Sometimes, when you look very hard for things, you think you see them even when they aren't there. Denny thought he saw some eyes looking back at him, but they were high up, above his head. They were framed in the low spreading branches of a

large oak, large brown eyes shining like lamps.

'I'm dreaming,' he thought. He looked down the hill towards the road, and back into the wood. The lamps had gone.

He heard a funny noise, like a whine.

'What are you?' he shouted – not too loud, because of Wayne. He felt nervous.

Nothing. Silence. A far-away cooing of pigeons, no longer frightened. Yet still the strong sense of being watched. Of a presence. It was a bit creepy, in spite of the fact he knew he wasn't frightened of the wood.

He walked on a bit, pretending he was unaware,

then turned suddenly and looked back. The branches of the oak were springing up and down, the leaves shaking, yet everything else was quite still.

'Who are you?' he said towards the oak tree.

Silence.

How stupid, he thought. He was imagining Waynes in the woods. All the same, he felt that it was real, whatever it was. An escaped lion perhaps? Should he be running? He hadn't heard of an escaped lion.

So occupied was he with this unexpected happening, he found he was walking down the hill back to the road without bothering about Wayne, and it came as a shock to remember what he was doing up there. He stopped in his tracks and dropped down out of sight from the road. Luckily, as it happened: Wayne was just coming out of his garden gate. Denny saw him look back up the road to see if his victim was in sight. Disappointed, he walked on towards school. Denny, farther away up the hill than the day before, sat like a mouse in the long grass until he was well out of the way, and then walked on slowly.

He got to school unmolested, but he was late. Wayne tripped him up in the school playground in break; apart from that it wasn't a bad day. When the bell went at the end of the afternoon, he sprinted out like an athlete and was half way home before Wayne had got out of the classroom.

As he got to where the footpath met the road, he decided to go home the same way, and see if there was any sign of a lion or elephant or whatever it was. Funny, he thought, that he was afraid of Wayne but a lion or an elephant seemed a whole lot less frightening. He liked animals. His dad was tractor man on the next farm, Paradise Hill, and sometimes he stood in for the cow man and Denny would go along with him, very early, long before school, and help bring the cows in. Perhaps there was a cow loose in the wood. If he found something interesting he might get a reward.

He walked as far as the oak tree and went into the undergrowth to search for clues. The bushes were much beaten down but there were no cowpats. Everything was quiet, save for the pigeons making their gentle calls, and a woodpecker drilling away in the distance.

Denny crashed around for a bit, but it was hot and there was nothing there; a few pigeons clattered away, but because of him, not a lion. The only clue he found was some fur caught in a quickthorn: it was gingerish and very long, about six inches. A Highland bull, he thought, thinking of a picture that hung in his Gran's bedroom in Wolverhampton. Too far from home.

The next day, he was ready in good time for school.

'Well, this is a change,' his mother remarked as he fetched his school-bag. 'Do you like it better now?'

'It's not bad sometimes,' he said cautiously.

His mother watched him go. He walked away down the road, and dodged back up the footpath when she had shut the door. He forgot all about Wayne, panting up the hill to look for the Furry Thing. He was half nervous, half excited. It was going to be another hot day. The wood was dark and cool and silent. He went as far as the oak tree and stopped.

Silence.

Perhaps it is asleep, he thought.

Perhaps it doesn't exist. There is nothing there.

He slipped past the oak tree and into the patch of beaten-down bushes. Then, on an impulse, he leapt on to a rotten branch so that it broke with a loud crack and shouted out, 'Where are you?'

There was a great flurry of cracking twigs ahead of him, and something huge reared up before his astonished gaze, covered with ginger fur. What it was he had no idea. He was so startled that he lost his footing on the mossy branch and fell in a heap – but if he

was startled, so was the Thing, for it was gone in a tremendous crashing of undergrowth, making strange strangled yelps of fear. As Denny lay with his heart banging like Big Ben he could hear the crashing of the beast's passage retreating deep into the trees far away. Who was the most surprised?

The creature, Denny thought, had been quite as terrified as himself judging by the speed of its flight – no lost domestic beast. But *what*? The glimpse Denny had seen did not fit with any animal he knew of. He got up and listened for a long time, but heard no more noises.

Whatever it was, it was as frightened of him as he was of Wayne. Somehow that made him feel sympathetic towards it, and want to help. He also felt that . . . somehow . . . if the grown-ups knew, they would have the same feelings about it as Wayne had about him, to catch it by surprise and capture it. Denny knew what that felt like.

That evening when his dad came home he said, casually, 'Are there any circuses around just now?'

'Not that I know of. Why, want to go?'

'I just wondered.'

A bear, he thought, it fitted with a bear, when you thought about it. A very big bear. But bears were dangerous.

'There aren't many about now,' said his dad.

'Why?'

'Oh, people got the telly, I suppose. Got used to smarter things.'

They weren't used to smart things, Denny thought,

18

even if they had the telly. His dad, for example, in his old red shirt and jeans, washing the dust off round the back of his neck with grampus noises in the kitchen sink, was nothing like as smart as Wayne's dad who went to work in a dark suit and drove a Mercedes. Wayne's dad smelled of aftershave, very strong. Once Denny had gone in Wayne's house because Wayne's mother had seen him with his knee all bleeding (after Wayne had thrown him over the stone wall – but she hadn't seen that bit) and taken him to put a plaster on it. She wasn't bad, but the house was so smart Denny couldn't imagine doing anything decent in it. Perhaps that was why Wayne liked to throw his weight about so much when he got outside. Thinking of Wayne – and he always seemed to be thinking about Wayne . . .

'Why am I so small? You're not.'

'Oh, don't start that again,' said his father wearily.

'Why though?'

'Search me. We asked the doctor and he said you'll grow soon.'

'Soon's been and gone.'

'We can ask him again if you like.'

His mother, frying bacon at the cooker, said, 'I read in the papers somewhere they say they can do something about it these days. They give you injections of something.'

'I don't want injections!'

'No. My way of thinking, when anything's new, how d'you know they'll get it right? Might give you too much and make you into a giant. Like they give

19

these women stuff if they can't have babies, and they have four or five.'

'How d'you like to be a giant then?' his dad asked, grinning.

Denny thought about it, especially meeting Wayne.

His dad said, 'There was a giant boy at school when I was a lad. Huge, he was. We all laughed at him – cruel we were, when I come to think of it. He was so big sitting in his desk, he couldn't get his knees under – they had to get a special table for him. And his mum couldn't afford him clothes – school uniform didn't come in his size. He had to wear right funny things from jumble sales.'

Denny pictured it in his mind. They laughed at him!

'When you laughed, why didn't he scrunch you?'

'Oh, he wasn't like that. He was huge, but he was very gentle. Too gentle for his own good, because he could have knocked us all for six if he'd wanted – when we teased him. But he never did. Just looked sad, somehow. You don't understand, when you're young, how people feel . . . I've often wondered.'

'What happened to him?'

'Oh, I dunno. He went away. I heard he couldn't get a job in town – he went on a farm somewhere. Worked as a forklift truck – by hand.'

His father laughed.

'You're still laughing at him,' his wife said.

'Well –'

'They laugh at me,' Denny said.

'Well, when they laugh at you, think of him, and think it could be worse.'

His mother came across to the table and gave him a friendly hug on the way. 'We could see about that treatment, if you like. I'm sure they know how to do it properly. I was only joking, what I said, about making you a giant.'

'No, I don't want that.'

He wished he could tell her about Wayne, but he

couldn't. If it wasn't for Wayne, he didn't care much really. Much better than being a giant! His dad's story made him feel quite grateful.

'Think,' his mother said, 'You're small but you're all there. You can run and see and hear, and laugh. You're bright. There's a lot worse off.'

Well, that was one consolation. Like at school dinner, when you left it and the ladies said, 'There's lots would be glad of that.' So they might, but it didn't change the fact that you yourself would puke up if they made you eat it. Or, when he got hit by a stone in the playground and his cheekbone got dented, they all said how lucky he was. How lucky he hadn't been blinded. But how could he have been *lucky*, when no one else got hurt at all? People did say some stupid things.

The conversation had gone off the point.

'Are there any Highland cattle round here?'

'No, lad. All Friesians, as I know of. Why?'

'Oh, nothing. I'm hungry.'

'You eat enough, I'll say that for you.'

At least his parents didn't fuss. There were some parents he knew about who fussed all the time. One boy had asthma and his mother fussed him nearly to death. It would be far worse if his parents fussed about his being small. If they did, he didn't notice it. It was only himself, and only – really – because of Wayne.

The next morning he was too late getting ready to go up by the footpath and had to take his luck along the road. He thought Wayne was ahead of him and went fairly slowly, but he was wrong. He had just passed Wayne's house when Wayne came out.

'Goodbye, darling!' Wayne's mother called from the door.

Denny wondered how anyone, even his mother, could call Wayne 'darling'. He came up, all shining clean just like his father, well-built and smart and exactly the right size, neither too large nor too small, handsome, with dark curly hair and large, pale blue eyes with long dark eyelashes that already the girls liked.

'Hullo, Dennis,' he said.

Nobody called him Dennis, except Wayne. Even the teachers called him Denny. He said it in a special way, with an emphasis that made it sound as bad as possible.

'Are you trying to avoid me, Dennis?'

'No.'

'I thought you were. I got something for you.'

Something nasty, no doubt. Denny shuffled along as fast as possible, anxious for the school gates. The others didn't bully him. He thought some of them even liked him quite, but didn't show it in front of Wayne, because they all knew Wayne wanted it that way.

'I've got you a present. It's in my pocket.'

'I don't want a present.'

'You do. It's a peppermint gobstopper. It's in a matchbox in my anorak pocket. If you put your hand in and open the matchbox, you can have it.'

'I don't want it.'

23

'You do, Dennis, really.'

He got up very close to Dennis and put his hand down on the back of his neck.

'Put your hand in and open the matchbox.'

Denny put his hand in and found the matchbox.

'No, don't pull it out. Open it and get the gob-stopper.'

Denny opened the matchbox and put his forefinger in. He touched something hard, thought for a moment that it really was a gobstopper, then a piercing pain burst the end of his finger and he screamed. He pulled his hand out and found a great stag-beetle fixed to the end of his finger, which hung on grimly as he flailed about. It was so horrible and

such a shock that he could not help screaming blue murder. It wouldn't let go.

An old man coming by on a bicycle stopped and shouted, 'What's up, lad?'

Denny roared. The man came over and Denny held out his hand.

'Ee, by gum, it's a long time since I saw one of those,' the man said.

He took hold of Denny's wrist and gently eased the great beetle's claws apart. It fell upside-down on the pavement and the man picked it up and put it right way up over the wall of someone's garden.

'How did that happen then?' he asked.

'It was on the pavement and he was poking it, teasing it,' Wayne said.

'Serves you right then, boy. It's one of God's creatures, same as you.'

He got on his bike and rode on.

Denny could not help crying, the shock had been so horrid. Wayne laughed.

'There, there, duckums, nasty thing got you, did it?'

Denny swung out with his school-bag as hard as he could, in a rage, but Wayne caught it, snatched it off him and flung it far over the nearest garden so that it landed with a crash against the glass front door. Denny gave a roar and rushed up the garden path to get it, reaching the front door just as the man of the house came to see what had knocked.

Denny snatched it up and the man caught him by

the arm and said, 'What's all this larking about? — could have smashed the glass, that could!' His face was very close and angry. Denny wriggled and squirmed, choking back tears. Wayne stood smugly by the garden gate.

'He threw it!' Denny shouted. 'It wasn't me. He threw it!'

But Wayne wasn't in the man's grip and could afford to grin. The man flung him off the doorstep and said, 'I'll remember your face, don't you worry. I'll be up and see the headmaster if there's any more of it.'

Denny scooted off back to the road, trailing his bag. This is where he would gladly have launched himself at Wayne and fought him with all his fury, but by past experience he knew that he could not win. Wayne would hold him at arm's length with one hand and taunt him until Denny would almost choke with rage. It had all happened many, many times before. Denny ran as fast as he could for school, but Wayne loped along behind him calling out, 'Is Dennis upset then? Poor little fellow, poor little diddums.'

By the time they got to school Denny was in such a rage he thought he would burst. But he couldn't go in crying and gibbering in front of everyone, especially as Wayne stopped within sight of school and wasn't to be seen when Denny arrived amongst his mates. Denny flung through and went into the toilets to regain his composure. Or would he ever? He was so wild. His finger was red and stinging still. What his father had said about the giant came into his mind, and he wished – whatever he had said last night – that he could come out of the toilets ten feet tall and pick Wayne up in one hand and toss him into the kitchen dustbins.

He was cast down all day, still reliving the beastliness of the stag-beetle latched on to the end of his finger, and ran out early before Wayne when the bell went, haring as fast as he could for home. But there was no pursuit, and it was hot, and when he got to the footpath turn he remembered the Thing, and decided to walk that way again. As he expected, there was nothing there today. All the same, he went into the flattened undergrowth to look.

It was hot again and quiet, and he felt he needed such peace to calm his disturbed spirits. The Wayne thing was getting unbearable. He did not know what to do, his life being ruined. He sat on the broken branch and picked at the green moss, soft and silky, that had grown in the crevices of the bark. He sat there quite a long time.

Then, slowly, he had the feeling that he was being watched again, as he had on the first day. There had been some soft rustlings farther into the wood which he had been too preoccupied to take much notice of. Now, suddenly, he heard a soft whining noise. He looked up. Through the undergrowth he saw two eyes watching him, huge and brown and soft, surrounded by long ginger fur. The leaves covered up all the rest of the thing; he could see nothing else. Or was it his imagination? He found he was trembling

slightly. The idea of its being a bear was a bit
different from even a Highland bull. Perhaps it
was the end of his perfect day – getting eaten by a
bear.

But somehow, it was strange to explain it, but he
felt a friendliness coming through the unblinking
gaze. Not only that, but a sadness, a longing.

'What are you, giant thing?' he said out loud, but
gently.

He dared not move. He might have it all wrong.

A very soft whimper.

He got up. The eyes disappeared. He looked up,
terrified, and saw them again way above his head,

about six feet off the ground, and a great mountain of fur arching out of the brambles. He gave a stifled scream – he could not help himself – and there was a great humping and crashing of cracking under-growth and branches and the Whatever-it-was turned and ran. Not quite so fast, but fast enough. Denny saw a great long hairy tail twitch through the close stems of the Forestry Commission pine trees and then the darkness in the pinewood swallowed it up.

A tail! Bears don't have tails, Denny thought.

He felt very shaken, but still not as frightened as he should have been. He had had a much better look at it this time, and it looked for all the world like a great hairy dog. But dogs didn't come that huge, even in circuses.

He went home very slowly, thinking.

'Whatever's wrong with you?' His mother asked when she saw him. 'You do look peaky! Like you've had a fright. Are you all right, love?'

Whatever would she say if she met that Thing? She'd go peaky all right.

Somehow, it was like Wayne, he didn't want to tell his parents about the Thing. It was his Thing. It liked him. It was lonely. It wanted him. But it was fright-ened. A lot of adults – if he said anything – would go looking with guns and pitchforks, if he gave them an accurate description. That wasn't what he wanted at all.

Whatever should he do?

He couldn't think about anything else.

His mother looked at him to see if he had any spots. 'There's chicken-pox going about,' she said.

The next time, he thought, he would not show any fright, and he would show the thing he was friendly too.

The next day he went early by the footpath but there was no sign of any movement in the wood. He hid from Wayne behind the wall, and was late for school but, after school, a teacher kept him talking and he had to go out at the same time as Wayne. Once clear

30

of school, the road being empty, Wayne put his arm round Denny's neck and clamped his head down under his arm, and walked along pulling him after him. Denny tried biting but only managed to get a mouthful of smelly anorak and pullover, then Wayne started hitting him over the head with his spare hand. Denny got one leg forward and managed to get it round Wayne's ankle and they fell over in a heap on the pavement. At that moment a car drew alongside with a loud hooting. It was Wayne's dad.

'Whatever are you two up to?'

'It's Dennis. He tripped me up, dad.'

'I thought you were fighting, by the look of it.'

'He wanted me to show him some judo holds, but he doesn't fight fair.'

'Nip in the car then, and you cut along, Dennis, and keep your hands off my lad.'

Dennis made faces after the car, retrieved his bag and headed up to the wood. His ears were still singing after Wayne's clamping hold. He wanted a friend.

He went into the wood and shouted, 'You great big, hairy thing, come out here! It's me, Denny. I'll give you a Mars bar.'

He sat on the log and considered the Mars bar, much squashed and tattered. He opened it at one end and couldn't resist taking a small bite, although he had promised it to the Hairy Thing. He knew it took patience to be a lion tamer, and supposed that it would take patience to become friendly with the Thing. Unless it ate him . . .

After a bit, he took another bite, quite small. Better

not eat too much, else to get the Mars bar, the Thing would *have* to eat him.

'I know you're in there. At least, I suppose you're in there. You haven't gone away, have you?'

It was quiet and still. Then, in the shadows under the pine trees, a wary movement. Denny froze.

A huge shape, bigger than a bear . . . As he looked, the great shape settled lower, crouching. To spring? Denny felt his mouth go dry with fear. He kept quite still. The thing was about the playground's width away, with bracken and blackberry bushes in between, still in the dark shadow of the trees. Something behind it was waving, like one of the besom brooms they kept in the fire-breaks to beat the flames with. It was a tail! Denny stared, open-mouthed. The Thing was wagging its tail! Denny couldn't believe it. It was for all the world like a great big dog.

He got up, very slowly, feeling rather shaky. Dogs never came that big?

'Do you want a Mars bar?' he called out. His voice sounded very queer. He went and stood out in the bracken. Although he was frightened, in a way, he also had a funny feeling that the animal was friendly. He stood boldly, very brave, holding out the Mars bar.

'Good dog, I'm a friend.'

The dog slowly shambled to its feet and stood without moving. It was as high as Wayne's dad, and looked like a giant old English sheep dog, save that it was ginger, and it had a very long tail. Its nose was slightly pointed but its forehead broad, with

scrumpled ears sticking out of a heavy tangled fringe, and huge, anxious, brown eyes. The tail was waving slowly from side to side, making a breeze across the bracken.

Denny stood, not knowing what to do, too excited now to be frightened. He had never seen a dog like it, so huge it was bigger than a pony, as big as a cart-horse, he supposed. He reckoned he could almost walk under its tummy without bending his head.

Slowly, he took the rest of the paper off the half a Mars bar and, very cautiously, he took a few steps towards the dog.

'Come on, Harry.'

He had always thought, if he had a dog, he would call it Harry.

Harry's nose twitched. He did not retreat but he lay down again, very expectant, head up, watching. Denny walked up to him. The Mars bar disappeared in a flash, but Denny's hand was still there. A great pink tongue as big as a pillow-case came out and slopped at his face, nearly knocking him over.

Denny was entranced. It was as if the dog, lying down, was aware that it frightened people, trying to be gentle but really, he could see, terribly pleased to see him. An ordinary dog would have jumped up, but this dog lay down, because it knew it was the best thing to do. It wriggled and made little panting, whimpering noises in its excitement, and its tail waved like one of the fir-trees in a high wind.

'Where've you come from?'

It wore no collar. Nobody made collars that big.

'What we going to do then?'

Whatever would happen if he took him home? Mum would have a fit. What was he living on, if he was a stray? The wood was full of rabbits, so Denny supposed rabbits. What was going to happen to him?

Denny put his hand on the thick hairy coat and stroked the dog's head, reaching up as best he could. Probably the dog didn't feel a thing. But his bright eyes watched, full of excitement and pleasure and the

great tongue licked at Denny, soaking him to skin.

'Hey, lay off!' It was like his mother flannelling him in the bath.

Denny didn't know what to do.

'I'll have to tell my dad about you. He'll know what to do. I can't take you home. My mum'll faint.'

He stood talking for a bit, and Harry twitched and snuffled, and tried not to lick him, although he obviously wanted to. His great body was all a-wriggle with excitement and pleasure and his tail had swept a great hole in the undergrowth, down to the leafy soil.

Now that he had befriended him, Denny did not think he could leave him here in the woods. But equally, he thought he would have to prepare the way at home. He must talk to his dad.

'You're not to follow me,' he said sternly. 'I'll come back, but you're to stay here.' He backed off and said, 'Stay!' very sternly, like a proper dog-trainer.

Harry seemed to droop, his tail falling flat and still. The anxious look came back into his eyes. Very bright, they were fixed on Denny. Denny said, 'I will come back, I promise.'

He started to walk away backwards. Harry half got up and he said, 'Stay!' again, very gruffly, and Harry settled back. Denny felt terribly mean leaving him. 'I promise I'll come back, I promise!' he called out.

He ran all the way home. He was very excited; he felt breathless. He was sure nobody, but nobody, had ever come across such a find as Harry.

His mother said, 'Good gracious, you look as if you've got a temperature!'

'I haven't!'

He didn't want to tell his mum, only his dad. His mum would carry on, but his dad knew about animals and would come and look, Denny was sure. His dad would decide what to do. But his dad was very late home.

'He's gone up to Price's to help mend the roof. He won't be back till late.'

Denny had to go to bed before his father came home. He supposed another day wouldn't hurt, but felt very anxious. In the morning there was no chance to talk to him – he was in a hurry and Denny had lost his homework. All was chaos. There wasn't even time to run up to the woods, just sprint along the road. Wayne could be seen way ahead, hurrying, late as well, so Denny was in the clear for a change.

The day at school seemed to drag interminably. Denny could think of nothing but that amazing dog waiting for him up in the woods. He just knew it would be there. He bought two Mars bars at lunchtime and put them away in his school bag. When the bell went he sped off, not giving Wayne a thought. He ran down the road and turned up the footpath. The hurry had given him a stitch and he had to slow down, but not too much. He could not wait to see Harry again.

He got to where the footpath bent round so that it ran parallel to the road and walked more slowly along the top towards the big oak tree and the clearing behind it where he knew – hoped – Harry

would be. He realized he felt nervous again. His heart was beating hard, not only with running. Suppose Harry wasn't really as tame as he seemed? Even being licked by him was fairly dangerous. He wanted to be friends with Harry so badly, that now he was nearly there, he was frightened something might go wrong.

'Gotcha!'

Half-frightened anyway, standing there under the oak tree, he nearly jumped out of his skin at the great shout in his ear. He spun round just as Wayne jumped over the wall from the other side of the path, and knocked him over with his school-bag.

'There, you didn't know I was there, did you? Didn't know I knew you came this way? There's no way you can escape me, Dennis!'

He flumped down on Denny, pinning him down on his back. His cocky, handsome face was all laughs and triumph. Denny could not move. He *hated* Wayne! His lovely, exciting moment, that he had looked forward to all day, blasted by the eternal Wayne who delighted in making his life a misery.

'It's not fair!' he cried out in despair.

'What's not fair, Dennis? Of course it's fair – a little, squitty, nitty, pin-headed, skinny minnow like you . . . you shouldn't be alive at all, you're so titchy. If you were a tomato you'd have been thrown out. If you were an animal you'd be put down. You're so *little*, Dennis darling, mummy's little, icky diddums pet –'

Denny knew it all off by heart, having heard it so many times before. He shoved with all his strength but could not budge Wayne's great hams off his chest. He could feel the tears of rage welling up behind his eyeballs, but knew he mustn't cry. Crying set Wayne off on another triumphant wave of taunting. But the rage was quite terrible, making him want to burst. He lashed out but Wayne caught his wrists, as usual. Denny could do nothing. He started to shout and scream.

'I hate you! I hate you! I wish you'd die!'

'Naughty Dennis,' smiled Wayne. 'That's not nice at all. God is listening. He'll put a black mark down – it's very naughty to wish people to die.'

Struggling with such effort, Denny thought he'd die of exhaustion – Wayne, he knew, was going to die of old age at about ninety. There would be no let-out for him. He slumped back, defeated, and as he lay on his back held hard by Wayne, he saw the familiar anxious brown eyes peering out from behind the oak tree. Unheard in the melee, Harry had come out to see what was going on. As Denny watched, the great dog shook himself free of the brambles and came out into the open, standing right behind the unsuspecting Wayne.

'Harry, help me!' shouted Denny.

He could see quite clearly that Harry was not quite sure what was going on. But, ever amiable, he put out his great tongue and licked Wayne's back.

Wayne's expression of glee turned to sudden surprise.

'What –'

He turned his head and saw the great wall of Harry's hairy chest close behind him. His eyes followed up and came to Harry's open mouth and his row of teeth as big as tea-trays hovering high over his head, and he let out a scream that Denny reckoned could be heard back at school.

His face turned the colour of putty. Denny thought his wish about him dying was actually going to come true, so quickly did he appear to shrink and shrivel up and wither with fright. His scream ended in a gulping sob, and then 'Denny, save me!' – a quivering whisper, and he threw himself down beside Denny, burying his face in his hands.

Denny was quite surprised.

He got up and said, 'Good old Harry. Want a Mars bar?'

He scrabbled for the Mars bar in his bag and peeled the paper off. Harry stood with his great tail sweeping backwards and forwards putting up a cooling breeze. Denny put the Mars bar on his tongue and Harry swallowed it with obvious delight, his body making his funny wrigglings and dipping of pleasure. His eyes shone with his anxious desire to be friends.

Denny stroked him, standing on tiptoe. His coat was like one of those goat rugs they sold on the market.

Harry, obviously concerned about Wayne, bent down to lick him some more.

'Help! Help me, Denny – help!'

Wayne was blubbering with fright so hard Denny thought he was going to pass out. He was about to tell him not to be so stupid, when it occurred to him that he had a very good opportunity to make the most of the situation.

'I'll keep my dog off you if you do as I say.'

'Please!'

'Just go away and leave me alone. And if you tell *anyone* about my dog, I'll set him on you. He could eat you with one mouthful.'

He paused to see what effect his pronouncement would have. Very encouraging. Wayne started to crawl – yes, crawl – away backwards.

'I'll keep him off you while you go.'

'Yes, Denny. Please!'

'And if you tell anyone – remember, I'll send him to get you.'

He thought he might have overdone it, as Wayne looked as if he was going to faint. Denny thought, I bet his mother'll think *he* looks peaky when he gets home.

'Off you go!'

The reversed situation slightly went to his head. He followed the crawling Wayne along the path, thoroughly enjoying his new role. He could see how very easy it could be to be a bully, if having the upper hand came so easily.

'Up you get, Waynie, run along now. But don't tell mummy! Or else –'

Wayne stumbled to his feet, took one anguished look at Harry and ran. He ran so fast, blindly, that he fell over about six times before he got to the road. Denny watched with a sense of incredible lightness and happiness. He, in his time, had run like that from Wayne, and knew only too well the agony of fear and frustration. Could it be true – could it really happen – that Wayne would stop persecuting him? The idea made him tremble with happiness.

He turned back and hugged Harry – except that his arms only went about a quarter of the way round him.

'I don't believe it!' he said. 'You are wonderful.'

Harry seemed to agree, wriggling and waggling and making friendly noises.

'But what am I going to do with you?'

The Wayne incident was extra, really. It had distracted from the business of the day, which was to decide how he could look after Harry. Harry was, after all, a stray dog, but not one which he could just take down to the police station. He wouldn't even go through the door.

Harry obviously wanted to follow his new friend home. Denny wondered if his father would be back – he was quite often early when he started very early, which he had today. He just had to have his dad's help.

He let Harry follow him halfway down the hill,
and then he turned and said to him very sternly,
'Stay here.'

Harry lay down and looked at him with his head
cocked on one side, eager and obedient. He blocked
up the whole footpath, his sides touching the walls
on each side. Lucky no one used it much.

'Wait.'

His dog-training voice was slow and stern. Harry
wagged his tail, felling all the cow-parsley in the
immediate area.

Denny walked on with cautious looks over his
shoulder, but Harry was doing as he was told. He put
his head down on his paws and watched Denny
disappear round the corner. Denny sped along the
road and into his house. His dad was drinking a cup

of tea and reading the newspaper in the kitchen.

'Dad, I've found something! Come and look.'

'What is it then?'

'I can't tell you. You've got to come. *Please!*'

'Now just let him drink his tea in peace,' his mother said. 'He's only just come in.'

'It won't wait.'

'It'll wait while he gets his tea.'

Would it? Denny sincerely hoped so. He looked out of the front window but there was no sign of Harry. Suppose someone else looked up the pathway and saw him? Harry was his dog.

He stood by the kitchen table, hopping from leg to leg with impatience.

'Gracious me, what's it all about?' his mother asked. 'Found a fortune or something?'

'Hurry, dad. Please, dad.'

'Stone the crows! What's got into you?' His dad downed his cup of tea and stood up. 'It's not far, I hope?'

'Just in the lane. Round the corner.'

'Lead on.'

Denny led. They rounded the corner into the footpath and Harry, seeing them, stood up and barked with joy.

'It's all right, dad – honest!' Denny cried out, seeing the look on his dad's face. He did not look very different from Wayne, half-an-hour earlier.

'God in heaven, Denny!' He clutched Denny's arm and took several paces backwards, gaping at Harry.

'Honest, dad, he's nice, not a bit savage.'

Certainly Harry looked the picture of friendliness, waggling away, his big floppy tongue hanging out.

'I don't believe it! I'm seeing things.'

Denny explained all about how he had come to find Harry (leaving out the bit about Wayne) and as Harry stood there being as nice as Denny promised he was, Denny's dad gradually got over his fright and started to wonder the same things as Denny.

'Whatever are we going to do with him then?'

'I thought – thought –'

'He must be from a circus or a zoo or something.'

'I want him,' Denny said.

'Want him? What, for a pet?'

'Yes, I do.'

His father laughed.

'He's hungry, dad. We can't leave him here, can we? Please, please can't we take him home? While we think what we're going to do.'

'Does what he's told, does he?'

'Yes, he's ever so obedient.'

'Poor old fellow.'

Denny saw that his father too recognized the longing, anxious look in Harry's eyes, how badly he wanted to be looked after.

'I suppose he could go in the barn, while we find out where he's come from . . .'

Denny knew his dad wouldn't fail him. His dad liked animals too, and understood about them, working on the farm.

'Come on, Harry,' Denny said.

'Your mother'll die when she sees it.'

'We'd better warn her.'

Denny's dad went on ahead, and Denny reached up and put his hand in the goaty fur and walked Harry home. He had never felt so happy and relieved in all his life. There was nobody about luckily, and they went down the road and into the yard without anyone seeing them. Their house was one of a pair of farm cottages and at the side was a very large old threshing-barn, where Dad kept his tractor. The tractor was parked outside, and Denny led Harry into the barn. It was high and cool, with old wooden arched beams holding up the roof. Bales of hay had broken and split over the years and made a thick comfortable bed.

'Lie down,' Denny said in his dog-trainer's voice.

Harry lay down on the hay. He rolled over on his back and put all four legs in the air and wriggled and wagged his tail. It was an amazing sight. Then he barked with pleasure. Denny put his hands over his ears.

'Hey, none of that.' It sounded like a jet-plane dive-bombing.

'I'll get you some water.'

He fetched a bucketful and Harry drank it all up. Denny thought about feeding him with those tins of stuff you bought in the grocer's, but one tin would only be the equivalent of a small biscuit, he thought, to the great acreage that was Harry's tummy.

'Dad'll see to it,' he said to Harry.

His dad came back with Denny's mother, who went white when she set eyes on Harry.

'Oh, Brian, whatever is it? Wherever has it come from?'

Having been well warned, she did not faint, but Denny could see she was terrified.

'Honest, mum, he's really nice, not a bit fierce.'

Denny did his hugging demonstration and got drenched with an affectionate licking. His mum's eyes goggled. 'Oh, Brian, we can't possibly keep him!'

'He can stay here. He's all right here. He likes it,' Denny said anxiously.

'If you tie him up, he'll pull the barn down if he decides to go.'

'He won't go. He wants us, can't you see? He wants somebody to be friends with him.'

Harry lay down and gazed with longing at Denny's mum, making exactly the right effect. Although he was so huge, he had a pathetic quality which Denny could see, having captured him, was having the same effect on his parents.

'Poor old boy then,' said his mother.

Harry wagged his tail, so that the dust flew.

'Hey, steady on.'

'Whatever are we going to feed him on?'

Denny's dad said, 'I daresay I could get something from Nick.'

Nick, Denny remembered, was a wholesale butcher who his dad met at market when he went in with some animals from the farm.

'We can keep him then?'

'He can stay tonight, until we find out where he's come from. I'll see if I can get him a meal or two from Nick.'

'Oh, Brian, we'd better not say . . . I mean, if people see him, they'll be ever so frightened.'

'I'll say! I nearly died.'

Denny could see that his parents were excited, underneath the doubt – feeling, like him, that Harry was quite something as a pet. His dad went off to see Nick – 'I won't tell him just how big it is – I'll say it's just a big stray that's walked in.' Denny shut the gate, but Harry seemed quite happy to stay in the barn. He lay with his nose on his paws, looking out of the door. He could have gone out and stepped over the gate without any trouble if he had wanted to disappear.

'Whatever are we going to do with him?' Denny's mother kept saying. Denny wanted to keep him, but thought it wiser not to say so – yet.

When he went to bed he could see Harry from his window, eating the enormous bones his dad had brought him, very happy. Denny snuggled down, thinking back to the glory of Wayne grovelling in the dust saying, 'Help me, Denny!' It was like a dream come true, Harry causing this wonderful situation to come about. Denny thought that, instead of Harry, he ought to give him a wonderful name, like Froggett's Revenge, the sort of name that dogs had who won prizes at Crufts. He dreamed of taking him to a Dog Show, entered as Froggett's Revenge, and how everyone would fall back and gasp with amazement when he entered the ring, with 'Revenge' trotting obediently beside him.

He woke very early. Remembering Harry, he lay blissfully thinking that he no longer had to endure Wayne's tortures. The thought was as good as all the treats he could think of rolled into one, as good as waking up on the first day of the school holidays. While he was lying there, his dad looked round the door.

'You awake, Denny?'

'Yes.'

'How about taking our dog for a walk, before there's anyone around?'

Denny leapt out of bed and flung on his clothes.

'I thought we could go in the Landrover, take him up the fields. He can't stay in the barn for ever.'

It was a fine morning, the hills shining with dew and skylarks flying up out of the ripening barleyfields. There was a wide farm-track up beyond Denny's cottage which led out into large fields of cow pasture, ideal for running a great dog like Harry. They drove out, Denny opening the gates as they went and shutting them again after Harry had bounded on ahead. The idea of taking the dog for a walk with the Landrover was ideal, for on the flat bits they could almost keep up with him as he bounded joyfully over

the grass, tail streaming, looking like some extraordinary flying haystack. He ran circles round them, and galloped back to the Landrover to cover it in great pink licks of joy.

'Good as a carwash,' said Denny's father.

When they got home, Harry went happily into the barn and settled down to his bones.

'You stay there till I come home,' Denny said sternly.

Harry swept the floor with his tail, sending up clouds of dust. His eyes shone with gratitude.

'What a dog, eh?' said Denny's dad.

They went into breakfast, and then there was the bliss for Denny of starting off for school without having to watch for Wayne. He walked boldly down the road and past Wayne's gate. Just after he had passed, Wayne came out of the front door. His mother was with him.

'What's the matter, darling?' Denny heard her say.

Wayne mumbled something.

'Hurry up now, or you'll be late.'

Denny waited, so that Wayne came out of the gate and had to catch him up.

'Hullo, Waynie. Mummy's diddums a bit sickly this morning then?'

Wayne scowled at him.

'My dog's longing to have a go at you,' Denny said cheerfully.

Wayne gibbered, 'Honest, I won't touch you again. I promise, Denny.'

'Okay. You know what, if you do.'

Denny swaggered on towards the school gates, feeling as if he were walking in the clouds. His whole life was transformed. After school, he ran home all the way, to see Harry. In the evening he went up the fields again, with his father, taking Harry for a walk.

'I've asked around, but no one's heard of any big dog gone missing. I went to the police, and they don't know. I didn't say how big, mind you. Just big, I said.'

'Can we keep him, if nobody wants him?'

'Well, I dunno, Denny. I'll get a licence for him, to be on the right side, but I dunno what to do really.'

'Please can't we keep him!'

'For now, I daresay. I want to see him right as much as you. But –'

'The work!' Denny's mother said. 'Every time he wags his tail there's like a dust-storm across the garden, all over the washing. His coat's a disgrace, all matted and full of mud, and how are you going to clean that, I'd like to know?'

'That's right, he could do with a good old clean-up,' Denny's dad said thoughtfully. 'Perhaps we could do that.'

'How, dad?'

'It's hot enough . . . perhaps, if we take him down to the river –'

'We could go on Saturday?'

'Why not?'

On Friday night Denny helped his dad fill the Landrover with buckets, scrubbing-brushes, a step-ladder and a large can of detergent and early the next morning they drove across the fields and past the farm to where the track crossed a bridge over the river. Denny's dad parked on the bridge.

'Come up then, Harry – in you go!'

He leaned over the parapet with a big juicy bone in his hand and Harry slithered down the bank and into the water and waded out for the bone. The water came up almost to the top of his back. When he was nice and wet Denny called out again, and his dad set up the step-ladder and while Denny kept him still, talking to him at the front end, his dad started to lather and scrub him. Harry liked it, and was quite happy to stand still in a cloud of bubbles, while Denny waded in and out fetching buckets of water for his dad to tip over Harry from the top of the ladder. By

the time he had finished they were both soaked
through and dripping and exhausted. Harry stood,
somewhat dejected, looking strange and flattened,
and shivering slightly.

'Come on!' Denny's dad flung everything back in
the Landrover, backed off the bridge and drove away
at a rate of knots, so that Harry had to gallop flat out
to keep up. Round and round the fields he went,
several times, so that Harry's dripping coat flew up in

the warm morning air and by the time they got home it was dry and shining. They stood him in the yard and brushed him with the yard brush (washed clean first) and combed him with the garden rake, so that by the time they had finished his coat was several shades paler and shone like gold, lying smooth and shining to amazing effect.

'Well I never, isn't he beautiful!'

Denny's mum couldn't believe it. 'Why, he'd win

any dog show, looking like that. Nobody could beat
him.'

'What class? He isn't any breed that I know of.'

'They have other classes, not just breeds,' Denny
pointed out. '"The dog the judge would most like to
take home" –'

'Well, count him out of that.'

'"Largest dog" – they do have that sometimes.'

'We'd win that all right.'

They got the local paper out and looked at all the
Coming Events. Being midsummer, there were plenty
of fetes, horse shows, dog shows and strawberry teas
and, amongst the list, they found a class for 'Largest

Dog' (and 'Smallest Dog') at the show in the next village.

'How about it then?'

They all looked at each other, thinking of the impression Harry would make.

'Be a bit of fun, wouldn't it?' Denny's mother said.

'I could borrow the cattle truck, to take him. The guv'nor wouldn't mind.'

'What about a collar and lead?'

They started to work out a plan. The show was the next day, in aid of Church funds. Denny went and borrowed a stirrup-leather from a horsey girl down the road to use as a collar, and his father produced a bit of shiny chain that restrained the farm-dog where he worked, and the cattle truck which they all hosed out and filled with straw. Harry watched them with interest from the barn, his head cocked on one side and his eyes shining out from beneath his gleaming fringe. He gently waved his tail and the long hair hung down like a silk curtain.

'What a beauty! There's no one will beat us.'

Best of all, Denny thought as he went to bed, Wayne's parents owned a very smart Great Dane which they entered at Kennel Club shows, and he was pretty sure they would have it at the fete the next day, confident of taking the prize for Largest Dog.

They all drove out in the cattle-lorry with Harry in the back and arrived at the show in good time. It was warm and the place was crowded, with dogs of all shapes and sizes (except Harry's) barking and getting tangled up in their leads.

'You go and enter him for Largest Dog then,' Denny was told. 'And get a number.'

Denny went to the Secretary's tent and waited in the queue. When it was his turn he offered up his entry money and asked for Largest Dog.

'Dog's name?' asked the lady briskly.

'Froggett's Revenge,' said Denny.

'My word!' said the lady.

She gave him his number and he went back to his parents.

'You'd better wait till all the others are in the ring,' his dad said. 'Because if you go in first, none of the others'll bother to enter. They'll all want their entry money back.'

They went in the lorry and gave Harry a last brush and comb, and Denny fastened the 'collar' round his neck and attached the chain. His mother went to spy out when the ring was ready and all the other dogs were in. Denny tied his number round his waist.

'Come along!' They could see his mother signalling anxiously.

'Here we go then.'

Denny's father dropped the ramp at the back of the cattle-truck, and Harry walked proudly down and stood gazing about him.

'Come on, Harry.' Denny gave his lead a tug.

But as he started to move cries of astonishment could be heard on all sides, not to mention a few screams, and a crowd started to collect which blocked their way.

'Give 'im some room! Let 'im through!' Denny's dad shouted out, and he went on ahead, clearing a passage, while more and more people came surging up to have a look. By the time he had got to the ringside, even the children's sports had come to a halt, and all the ladies were streaming out of the tea-tent and the Flower-Arranging tent, and the Bowling-for-a-Pig had ground to a halt, and one of the ponies going down to the gymkhana shied with fright and threw its rider.

Denny followed his father, feeling slightly anxious. Funny, but having got used to Harry, he had rather forgotten his own fright on first setting eyes on him, and now he saw that they were causing considerable consternation. When he got to the entrance to the ring, a white-faced steward stepped back and said, 'Is that a dog?'

Harry leaned down and enveloped him with a friendly lick. Denny gave an anxious jerk on his collar.

'Lay off, Harry. People don't like it.'

He pulled him into the ring where all the other competitors came to a halt and stood with their jaws hanging open. Wayne was leading round the family Great Dane with a smug look on his face, as it was much larger than all the other dogs in the ring, but when he saw Denny he went pale, and his Great Dane sat down on its haunches and started to howl. One of the lady judges fainted, and the ambulancemen

had to come in to revive her. The other judge, a man in a bowler hat, came over and said, 'Look here, I say, I don't know if – if –'

'If what?'

'I mean to say – what is it?'

'A large dog. That's what you want, isn't it?'

'Course it is,' said a spectator. 'That's a winner, that is.'

Harry bent his head down to lick the judge, who did a quick move backwards and said, 'Lead on, lead on!'

Denny walked on and Harry sauntered at his side, wagging his tail in a friendly fashion, not pulling or being silly. The other big dogs gazed at him with expressions varying between suspicion and terror,

and Wayne's Great Dane took to its heels and fled, dragging Wayne behind it. Everybody was by now crowding to the ringside; there was a lot of shoving and pushing and a voice came over the loudspeaker, 'Will everyone keep calm, please. I appeal to everyone to keep calm!'

The judge came up to Denny with a certificate and a red rosette and said, 'Look, here's your first prize. Of course you've won. Now please take that animal out of here and *go away*. You're going to cause panic.'

Denny took the certificate and turned to go, slightly offended by the rebuff. But as he left the ring a big crowd clustered round him, including men with notebooks at the ready, reporters from the local newspapers, not to mention a policeman or two.

'Where did you get this dog, Mr Froggett?'

'Have you had it long?'

'What's its breeding, Mr Froggett?'

'How old is Froggett's Revenge?'

'Froggett's who?' said Mr Froggett.

'Have you got a licence for this dog, Mr Froggett?' said the policeman. 'And how did you come by it? I'm not sure that keeping a dog this size isn't against the law.'

'How can it be?'

'"Causing a public nuisance",' said the policeman.

'But it isn't.'

'Causing a public consternation, the judge to faint, for example.'

'Oh, come off it,' said Mr Froggett.

'I think we should have a word.'

Camera bulbs started flashing and popping, and Harry stood with his head up, posing like a film star, licking everyone within range.

'Doesn't he just love it?' said Denny's mum, who was rather enjoying it herself.

'Perhaps we'd better put him away,' said her husband, 'and go. I'm not so sure it's a good thing.'

'Can we have your address, Mr Froggett? I'd like to come along and interview you, if I may?'

'Well, I don't know –'

Denny's dad turned to Denny and said, 'Get him back in the truck, for heaven's sake, and I'll put the ramp up.'

The policeman said, 'And I'll have your address too, Froggett. I think we'll have to go into this.'

'Oh, Lor', what have we let ourselves in for?' said Denny's dad.

They loaded Harry back in the lorry, but the crowd would not go away, everyone peering and shoving and asking questions, so they decided to leave, to get a bit of peace. Going back in the lorry they couldn't help laughing at the upset they had caused.

'As long as the old busybodies don't start upsetting things,' Mr Froggett said, remembering the policeman's remarks.

'Well, we couldn't have kept him secret for very long,' his wife said. 'Besides, I'm sure I don't know if we can keep him permanently . . . think what he'll be like in the winter when it gets muddy, and you can't go on taking him for walks with the Landrover for ever. All that diesel it uses –'

They got home and fed Harry (having Nick the butcher for a friend was very useful) but before they could sit down and feed themselves, the telephone started to ring.

'Is that Mr Froggett? This is the *Daily Sun*. We understand you own a monster dog. Could we send someone down to talk to you? Tonight?'

'Mr Froggett? This is *Dog News*. I understand you have a very large dog of unknown breeding. We would very much like to interview you . . .'

'Mr Froggett, this is Symmonds Safari Park. We are interested in this dog of yours . . .'

'Hullo, this is Gerry Mander talking from Manders Circus. Word is going around that you are the owner of a very unusual dog. Is this true? Would you be available if I drive over to see you . . .?'

'Dear Mr Froggett, I really don't like to trouble you, but my name is Miss Flower and I'm arranging a Charity Dog Show at the end of the month and I wondered if by any chance you could bring this very unusual dog of yours? A sort of Celebrity appearance, you might say.'

'Froggett, my name's Smith. How much do you want for this dog of yours?'

'Froggett, this is Penny – I represent Animal Rights and The Vegetarian Group Against the Exploitation of Animals. Could I come over tomorrow and ask your views on keeping Unusual Pets and exhibiting them for gain?'

'Eh?' said Denny's dad.

After about ten calls he took the phone off the hook.

'I don't like this. We don't want all this stir, do we?'

'Looks as if we're going to get it, dear.'

Denny was worried. 'No one's going to take Harry away, are they?'

'We'll see that dog right, don't worry,' said his dad.

But Denny did worry. When he went to bed he lay wondering what was going to happen, all these people taking an interest, interfering. And his mum saying, 'I'm sure I don't know if we can keep him.' Even his dad hadn't promised they would keep him, only that he'd see him right. But a dog needed *somebody* to look after him, not a Safari Park or a circus. They might put him in a cage! Because he was too big to come in the house, Denny spent quite a time sitting talking to him in the barn, and Harry would watch and wait for him, and greet him with a big swoosh of his tail, and the very gentlest of licks, which he realized was more welcome than a big rough wet one. Sometimes he walked round the house and looked in at the windows, wriggling and waggling and wanting someone to come out and play. And Denny would go out and Harry would lie on his back with his paws in the air and bark a welcome. Denny knew Harry loved him and he wanted to be with him all the time. If only he was an ordinary-sized dog!

Denny lay wondering for a while if there was any way of making him smaller, like his mum had said the doctors had found a way of making under-sized children bigger, but he supposed it was unlikely. He didn't much care about being small now that he had

Harry and Harry had put Wayne in his place. Not having to worry about Wayne any more was blissful.

Next day Denny and his Dad took Harry round the fields very early, as usual, and then went to school

and work respectively, leaving Harry in the barn. But
when they got home there were cars parked outside
their house and a lot of people in the yard, all
crowding round Harry and Mrs Froggett, who was
looking rather short-tempered. Harry was looking

anxious, and greeted Denny with obvious enthusiasm – a joyful bark that sent the nearest spectators reeling.

There was no way of getting rid of all these people except by telling them all they wanted to know and letting them take photographs.

The next day the same thing happened. Mrs Froggett made tea and cakes and sold them at the gate, and Wayne's parents complained to the police about lowering the tone of the road, and the local policeman came down to follow up the complaint, and ate four slices of Mrs Froggett's chocolate cake.

'I don't know as this is right, mind you,' he said. But there didn't seem to be a law that covered a lot of people wanting to see a dog like Harry, so he just said he'd 'keep an eye on the situation'.

'Come for more chocolate cake, most likely,' said Denny's dad, which proved correct.

The next day a television team arrived to film Harry, and after he had appeared on television the postman brought a stack of Harry fan-letters, and even more people called to see him. The cars all got jammed up in the lane, and Wayne's father couldn't get home, and complained to the police again.

The policeman said, 'You showing your dog off like this, I reckon you ought to have an entertainment licence. Selling teas and all.'

'But we never invited them, did we? We'll stop the teas, if it's against the law.'

'Yes, I've had enough,' said Mrs Froggett. 'I thought it would all finish after a day or two. I'd like everyone to go away.'

'Easier said than done,' said the law. 'You've created a demand, like. You ought to sell the dog to a zoo or something.'

It was true that Mr Froggett had received many offers to buy Harry, from zoos as well as circuses, advertising agents, Guard Dog suppliers and various entertainment enterprises.

'But you can't let a dog like Harry go to a corporation. He had to belong to a person. Like he belongs to Denny now.'

'We're not selling Harry to anyone,' Denny said firmly.

'All the same,' Mrs Froggett said later at bedtime, when the crowd had dispersed. 'We can't go on like this.'

'We'll have to think of something,' her husband agreed.

Nobody wants Harry because he is so big, Denny thought, lying in bed that night. He couldn't sleep for worrying about Harry. It was true that taking him for walks with the Landrover was proving very expensive, and the mornings were gradually getting darker now that summer was getting on. It was also true that keeping him in the winter was going to be very difficult.

'I am the wrong person for Harry, because I am too small. Harry is so big he wants a very big owner. A giant.' Denny tried to work out a solution. A giant who lived in lots of space, where he could take him for giant runs.

Lying in bed, staring at the ceiling, Denny remembered his dad's story of the giant boy in his class at school, who was too big to sit at a desk and who wore old clothes from jumble sales because the school uniform didn't come big enough. That giant would be the same age as his dad now, if he had been in the same class.

At breakfast he said to his dad, 'You remember you told me there was a giant boy in your class at school?'

'Willie Little? Yes.'

'Willie *Little?*'

'Yes, that was his name. Why?'

For a moment Denny was thrown by the thought of a giant boy called Little, but then he remembered his idea and said, 'Where is he now?'

'I've no idea. Why?'

'I just thought –'

'Of course! I see what you think. You mean, he and Harry would – sort of, go together?'

'If we can't keep him, yes. Not for him to go to a zoo, I don't want that.'

'Nor me, mate. That's a very interesting idea. He was a nice chap. Never said much. Shy, he was.'

'You said he worked as a fork-lift truck.'

'Did I say that? I seem to remember he couldn't get a job indoors, like in an office, because the firms didn't want to buy new furniture and suchlike. I think he got a job on a farm, yes.'

They looked up Little in the telephone directory, but there was no W. Little there. 'Mind you, I don't see that he'd be on the phone, anyway. He wasn't a great talker.'

'We could ask the policeman. The police know how to find people.'

'Only if they're Missing Persons.'

'But he's not a Missing Person. Just because we don't know where he is doesn't mean he's missing. But they might know, that's a fact.'

They asked, but W. Little was neither missing nor wanted.

'If he worked on a farm, perhaps we could trace him through the National Farmers Union,' Denny's dad decided.

Denny pretended they were private detectives, hunting down an informer.

'High Tops Farm, Windhover. Willie Little, farm labourer,' said the National Farmers Union.

'That'll be him.'

'Can we go and see him?' Denny pleaded.

'Why not? He'll remember me, I daresay.'

They went the next Sunday, in the Landrover. The farm was about forty miles away, further into the hills and moors, a remote and very beautiful area where tourists went in summer. High Tops farm was high up a valley, at the end of a bumpy lane. The house was pretty, stone-built, surrounded by old cow-barns and some modern hay-barns behind. They drove up and parked the Landrover.

'Nice spot,' said Denny's dad.

Plenty of room, Denny thought. Harry could bound up the crags and gallop along the ridges with his long tail pluming out behind. No one to come poking and prying and nosing like at home.

They got out and went to the farmhouse and knocked at the door. The farmer came out, a pleasant-looking man who introduced himself as Mr Orchard.

'I'm looking for an old school-friend of mine,' Denny's dad said. 'A fellow called Willie Little. We were told he was working here.'

'Willie? That's right, he is.' Mr Orchard gave them both a shrewd, inquiring look. 'You know Willie's trouble then?'

'His size, you mean?'

'That's right. You won't get a shock, meeting him – like some?'

'No, I remember.'

'He lives here, works here, never goes out anywhere. He doesn't like to be seen out, the way people stare at him. It's a right shame. He has a hard time.'

Mr Orchard led them out into the yard. 'Come this way.'

They followed him through the cow yard into a yard behind, where there was a big Dutch barn. One end had hay in it and the other was blocked round with timber in clapboard fashion, with doors and windows set in. The doors were barn doors, about ten feet high.

'The only place we could think of for him to live,' said Mr Orchard.

He knocked on the door and shouted, 'Willie! Let's have a word.'

The door opened and Willie came out. Denny, having been warned, was all the same somewhat staggered at the sight of Willie, and stepped back anxiously. Willie was about eight feet tall, and put all his surroundings out of scale. The Dutch barn, from seeming enormous beside the rest of the buildings, suddenly seemed like a quite ordinary shed, with Willie standing in the doorway looking down on them. Denny felt that it was themselves that had shrunk, Tom Thumb-wise, as if by some sudden magic. Through the open door he could see a massive table and a bed to match, and on the table a teapot like they used at the Women's Institute for sports days and a wash-stand basin for a bowl. He could feel himself gaping, as the people at the show had gaped at Harry, but he couldn't help himself.

'You remember, me, Willie? Brian Froggett?'

Willie's great moon face broke into a smile. High above, Denny saw blue eyes bright as police warning lamps taking them in, friendly and warm. What an extraordinary man! His movements were slow and careful, as if he was afraid of breaking anything – indeed, it must be like living in a world of fragile eggs, Denny thought, moving amongst ordinary people. He was in no way frightening once the shock of his size had been overcome – he was so obviously friendly and gentle. He shook hands with infinite care, his huge fingers exerting the lightest of pressure.

'Very nice to see you again, Brian. Very pleased I'm sure.'

'And Denny, my son.'

'Pleased to meet you, Denny.'

He stood back in the doorway and gestured inside. 'Do come in, please.'

Denny saw at once that there was room for Harry in here, to lie on the hearth-rug in front of the stove that had been built in to one wall. On this scale, Harry would look quite normal. He would just be an ordinary house dog like lots of people had. Even if he wagged his tail, the massive table would stand firm.

'How did you find me here?' Willie was asking. 'I don't get around much you know.'

'We asked around,' Mr Froggett said. 'We had a special reason.'

He had cut out all the newspaper photos of Harry which had appeared in the local press, all of them emphasizing Harry's enormous size by posing him against something familiar, like the Landrover, or against the kitchen door. He put them down on the table and Willie and Mr Orchard looked at them with interest.

'Aye, we heard about this fellow,' said Mr Orchard. 'I saw him on the telly. Yes, that's right, I remember you now, lad.' Mr Orchard turned to Denny. 'You so little, handling this dog – it's a great story, I thought. I told you, Willie, didn't I? Told you there was a dog around like yourself, ten times bigger than everyone else.'

'That's right. And I remembered the name, Froggett. I wondered then if it was Brian Froggett, didn't I? He always liked animals, I said.'

'Well, fancy, you should have brought the dog with you. I wouldn't mind setting eyes on a dog like that,' said Mr Orchard.

'Well, it takes a cattle truck to move him. Run behind he would, but it might be against the law. But we did think, seeing as how the two of you are of a size, you might like him, Willie, to keep you company?'

'Hey, that's an idea,' said Mr Orchard admiringly. 'I always said you should have a dog for company, Willie, didn't I? Seeing as how you never go out and meet anybody. You want a bit of company.'

'Aye, well, they all stare and laugh at me, I get fed up with it,' Willie said.

'They wouldn't laugh at you if you had Harry with you,' Denny said emphatically.

'They stare at Harry, and he loves it. Licks them all, wags his tail and knocks 'em all over.'

'You bring the dog over, Mr Froggett,' said the farmer. 'And we'll see how we get on. You'd like that, Willie, wouldn't you?'

'I wouldn't mind a dog, aye,' said Willie.

They all went outside again. Mr Orchard and Denny's dad walked back towards the Landrover, but Denny stayed a few minutes with Willie.

'They teased me because I'm so small,' he said. 'But when I got Harry, they stopped.'

'Did they now?' said Willie thoughtfully. He sighed, like a gust of wind coming down from the hills.

Denny looked up at him. He had the anxious look

78

on his face that he remembered had characterized Harry's face when he had first seen him. His wide, honest face, in repose, was very sad and lonely, the light dull in the blue-lamp eyes.

'If it weren't for Mr Orchard taking me in, I don't know what would have become of me,' he said.

Denny had always thought giants could conquer the world. Willie, if he wanted, could decimate the likes of complaining Wayne's dad, crush his smart Mercedes in one kick with his foot.

'It's no good in this life, Denny,' he said. 'If you're different.'

Walking back after his dad, when he had said goodbye, Denny supposed that what Willie said had some truth in it: if half the people in his class were as small as he was, he wouldn't get bullied and teased. He only got bullied and teased because he was different.

'You're right, lad,' his father said when they were driving home. 'That's the way it is. Poor Willie, at school, had a terrible time. Just as well for us he wasn't a bad-tempered lad, else he'd have killed us. His mother was always on at him, to be quiet and gentle, else "they" would lock him up, so he was scared stiff of losing his temper. And now look at him – frightened to go out. I suppose I must take some of the blame, because I teased him too.'

Denny felt really sorry for Willie and the sadness at losing Harry was helped by the thought of his being good for Willie.

'I think he'd be happy with Willie, which is what

matters,' his dad said. 'We'll be sad to see him go, but happy if he finds a nice home. Happy if he's happy.'

When they got home Mrs Froggett said people had been calling all day, and a Safari Park had offered a thousand pounds for Harry, and a man from a seaside amusement park had promised to call back, with cash at the ready, if Mr Froggett would just name his price.

Denny looked anxiously at his dad, having heard him say so many times what couldn't he do with a thousand pounds.

To his relief, his dad said, 'Money's not everything.'

Mrs Froggett looked sad, and said no, she supposed it wasn't.

'Did you find Willie Little?' she asked.

'They're two of a kind, Willie and our dog. Like a pair of gloves – I reckon they belong to each other,' said Denny's dad.

For all it was what they wanted, Denny felt very cast down at the thought of losing Harry. But his dad said, 'Look, lad, it's what's best for the dog that matters. We don't want him to be a tourist attraction, do we? Up there, he'll have peace, and he'll be a great friend to Willie. And Willie needs friends, you can see that. If they take to each other, it'll be great. And it'll be all your doing, lad. You can feel proud of yourself. Great stuff.'

Denny went out to the barn and sat in the hay with Harry, and told him about Willie. Harry always listened, sitting with his head on one side, his eyes shining out from under his long fringe, one corner of his great tongue hanging out like a bathroom rug to air from a window-sill.

'You won't have to stay in a barn all day. You'll have all the hills to roam on, great long walks for miles and miles.'

They took him up the next weekend in the cattle truck. As they drove into the yard, Mr Orchard came out to meet them.

'Aye, we've been really looking forward to this. Let's have him out now, and we'll go and tell Willie he's here.'

They let down the back of the cattle-truck and Harry bounded out, leaping round them in excited circles, barking. Mr Orchard gaped. Harry lay down on his front end, his back end and plumy tail waving happily high in the air, and made friendly waggles and whimpers, trying to contain his pleasure.

'Struth! What a dog!'

They went round to the dutch barn and knocked on the door. Harry stood waiting, ears pricked up. Willie came to the door, opened it, and Harry stood before him – no longer an enormous dog, but a quite ordinary-sized dog standing beside his master, his nose at the level of Willie's outstretched hand. Harry licked the hand and looked up at Willie, as he had never been able to look up to a man in his life. Watching them, Denny saw the amazing blue glow light up Willie's eyes as he took in Harry; the giant man and the giant dog, it seemed to him, took to each other in a way that was almost visible. Afterwards he tried to

81

describe to his father how he felt that something
passed between the two of them – a sort of codeword,
as if they had both recognized a kindred spirit, and

his dad said, 'Yes, I felt that too. Like a jigsaw coming together.'

At the time, seeing that he was losing Harry – in spite of it being what they all wanted – Denny felt a dreadful pang of loss and jealousy that he could not quite hide. He felt suddenly lonely and deprived. Harry had become, quite literally, a very large part of his life.

'What a match, eh?' his father said, and brought his arm down across his Denny's shoulders. 'I reckon you and me'll get a little dog, Denny – what do you think about that? Seeing as we've got used to having one about. We're going to miss our Harry.'

This exciting thought stopped the lump of misery that was gathering inside him. He thought they could come and visit Willie and Harry with another dog, which would make a match all round. When Harry went inside with Willie, Denny saw that he was quite right about Harry fitting on the hearth-rug. He lay down in front of the stove as if he had lived there all his life, and he fitted perfectly, exactly in the right proportion to the table, the teapot and Willie's slippers that lay like a pair of rowing-dinghies pulled up on the beach.

Willie sat and stroked Harry and rubbed his ears and said, 'I've always wanted a dog, but it didn't seem fair on an ordinary sort of dog – like having a lap-dog, and I never did like lap-dogs. Can I take him for a walk and see if he'll follow me?'

'Why not?'

Willie went out across the yard and over the wall

in his stride and Harry went with him, out on to the
pasture that climbed up to the fells. Willie started to
run and Harry bounded after him, and together they
climbed up across the grass, over the stone wall and
up into the heather and bracken. Up and up, jumping
and bounding across the stony screes and up the
crags, scrambling, running, until the two of them
were on the skyline, silhouetted against the bright
sky, as if one of those giant men engraved in the

chalk on the flanks of a grass down had taken to life and climbed up and stood erect. Then, with a great yodel of joy that echoed all around the hilltops, Willie started to run along the ridge of the mountain, and Harry ran after him, his tail pluming out behind him and his wild barks of excitement thundering down the valleys like the sound of quarry blasting.

'Well, did you ever see such a sight?' said Mr Orchard, with great satisfaction. 'That's wonderful for Willie. That's the best thing that's ever happened to him.'

'It's cheaper than using the Landrover, I'll say that,' said Mr Froggett, and they went in for a cup of tea with Mr Orchard.

When Willie came back, his great face glowing with pleasure, Mr Orchard took a photo of him leaning on the cattle-truck with Harry beside him. Then Denny and his dad stood beside them and he took another photo.

'I'll get some prints done for you, Mr Froggett. We'll all remember this day.'

'Yes, Brian – it's the best present I could ever have imagined. You come back again and see us soon. Come to tea, and bring your wife.' Willie shook hands all round as Denny and his dad got back into the cattle-truck. Harry stood beside him, wagging his tail. He came up to the window of the truck and gave Denny a farewell lick.

Denny sniffed a bit as they drove home, but his dad said, 'We'll look for another dog, never you mind.'

It was very quiet without Harry, but much more

peaceful. All the crowds went away disappointed and the lane fell empty again. None of the Froggetts told anybody where Harry had gone, and Wayne said his dad said they must have sold him for a lot of money, and what a cheat it was to sell something that wasn't yours to sell.

'We gave him to a friend,' Denny said, indignant.

'Didn't think you'd got any,' said Wayne rudely. Without Harry, Denny was finding that Wayne was getting slightly bumptious again. But he thought there might be a way out of that, if they went to visit Willie again.

They went about a month later. Mrs Froggett came as well, and said she wanted to stop in the town before they got to the farm, to do a bit of shopping. So Denny's dad made a detour into the town and parked in the market square. They got out, and as they crossed on to the pavement they saw Willie and Harry coming down the street towards them. Harry was on a lead, and everyone was making way for the pair, not frightened or alarmed, but in a friendly way, saying, 'Hi, Willie! Good old Harry!' Willie saw them and came across, grinning broadly. Harry obviously knew them and wriggled and wagged and licked Denny. His coat was smooth and shining and he had filled out and looked fitter and stronger than they had ever seen him. Willie too seemed far livelier and more cheerful.

'I never liked to come down to town before,' he said, 'But now, with Harry, everyone likes to see him and we come down often and get a bit of shopping for Mrs

Orchard. It's made a difference to me, I can tell you. We got something for you back home too – you've timed it well. You get your shopping, and I'll be home much the same time.'

When they got to the farm he was already back, loping ahead of them up the narrow lane as fast as they could drive. He went into his barn and came out with a cardboard box and handed it to Denny.

'Look in there. We were keeping it for you.'

Denny looked. There was an old blanket and, curled up in its folds, a black and white sheepdog puppy asleep. A normal-sized puppy . . . as Denny put his hand in, it opened its eyes and put out a warm tongue to lick him – a tiny, neat tongue like a postage stamp.

'There, he'll be the right size, I reckon, when he's grown – neater than this fellow here.'

Denny lifted him out and held him and the little plumy tail wagged as hard as Harry's. He didn't know what to say, he was so pleased and surprised.

'Ah, now, that's a sensible dog,' his mother said approvingly. 'We'll manage that one fine. That's very kind of you, Willie.'

They had a splendid day, with a huge dinner Willie had prepared, and Mr and Mrs Orchard came in for cups of tea, and Mr Orchard brought the prints of the photos he had taken. Denny looked at the extraordinary sight of Willie standing with his head on a level with the top of the cattle-truck, and Harry sitting on his haunches beside him, both of them dwarfing the tiny shrunken figure that was

himself standing only half as high as the truck's
wheel.

'That's really good. Can I have a copy?'

'Of course, we got a set printed for you.'

When they set off for home, the new puppy went
to sleep on Denny's lap, and Denny was no longer
sniffy at leaving Harry. Nobody could be sorry at the
glorious, happy dog Harry had become, stretched out,
when they left, in his place on the hearth as if he had
lived there all his life.

'What you call fitting in,' said Mrs Froggett. 'Which
is more than he did at our place.' She turned round to
Denny – 'But this one . . .'

'He's going to get spoilt, I reckon,' said Denny's
dad.

Denny thought, 'I'll teach him right . . . to snarl at Wayne.' If his other plan didn't work, that is . . .

Going to school the next day, Wayne came out of his house calling, 'Wait for me, diddy Denny, then!'

Denny waited.

'I've got something to show you,' he said to Wayne.

'Oh yeah?'

'That dog I had, and that friend we gave him to, I've got a photo here. Want to look?'

He handed it to Wayne. Wayne took it and peered sneeringly at the picture. As his eyes took in the size of Willie with Harry sitting beside him, his expression changed to one of utter disbelief, and then of anxiety.

'I don't believe it –'

'That's my friend, the one Harry's gone to live with. He said he'd come down any time, if I had any trouble – don't know what he meant, exactly. I don't have any trouble any more.' He turned to pale Wayne and said, 'Do I?'

'No, Denny. Not any more.'

'Carry my bag then, just to prove it,' Denny said, and threw it at him. Hard.

Wayne hitched it on his shoulder.

'And my new dog – he's *vicious*,' Denny said with satisfaction.

He walked on to school, feeling really good, and Wayne followed him, not saying a word.

THE COMPUTER NUT
Betsy Byars

When Kate receives a message on her computer from a mysterious admirer, she hopes it's her secret crush, Willie Lomax. But she eventually discovers – no thanks to 'help' from her best friend Linda – that Willie is not the culprit. In fact, he turns out to be a resourceful computer sleuth when the two team up for hilarious close encounters with the alien comedian

THE WITCH-CHILD
Imogen Chichester

Meet Mr and Mrs Gumblethrush, a wizard and witch, and their daughter Necromancy, who escapes to the world of ordinary children – a really funny fantasy story.

DOLPHIN ISLAND
Arthur C. Clarke

Johnny Clifton had never been happy living with Aunt Martha and her family for the twelve years since his parents had died when he was four. So when an intercontinental hovership breaks down outside the house, he stows away on it!

THE SHEEP-PIG
Dick King-Smith

Fly, the sheep-dog, looked at her strange new foster child with astonishment. The little piglet she called Babe had been won at a fair by Farmer Hogget and was surely destined to be fattened up for the family freezer – yet here he was wanting to be a sheep! So Fly taught him everything she knew, wondering what would happen when Farmer Hogget noticed what was going on . . .

THE GHOST OF THOMAS KEMPE
Penelope Lively

What kind of ghost was it that had come to plague the Harrison family in their lovely old cottage? Young James sets out to find the answer in this delightfully funny story, which won the Carnegie Medal.

BAGTHORPES ABROAD
Helen Cresswell

Pendemonium reigns supreme in the Bagthorpe household – particularly when Mr Bagthorpe announces that they're all going Abroad. But Abroad (luckily for Jack and Zero the dog) turns out to be a cottage in Wales – and a haunted cottage at that.

THE FREEDOM MACHINE
Joan Lingard

Mungo dislikes Aunt Janet and to avoid staying with her he decides to hit the open road and look after himself, and with his bike he heads northwards bound for adventure and freedom. But he soon discovers that freedom isn't quite what he's expected, especially when his food supplies are stolen, and in the course of his journey he learns a few things about himself.

KING DEATH'S GARDEN
Ann Halam

Maurice has discovered a way of visiting the past, and whatever its dangers it's too exciting for him to want to give up – yet. A subtle and intriguing ghost story for older readers.

STRAW FIRE
Angela Hassall

Kevin and Sam meet Mark, an older boy who is sleeping rough up on the Heath behind their street. Kevin feels there is something weird about Mark, something he can't quite put his finger on. And he is soon to discover that there is something very frightening and dangerous about Mark too.